John W. Ashby

Alachua

The Garden County of Florida - its Resources and Advantages

John W. Ashby

Alachua
The Garden County of Florida - its Resources and Advantages

ISBN/EAN: 9783337100681

Printed in Europe, USA, Canada, Australia, Japan

Cover: Foto ©Andreas Hilbeck / pixelio.de

More available books at **www.hansebooks.com**

ALACHUA,

THE GARDEN COUNTY OF FLORIDA.

ITS RESOURCES AND ADVANTAGES.

ISSUED BY THE

ALACHUA COUNTY IMMIGRATION ASSOCIATION.

THE SOUTH PUBLISHING COMPANY,

ENGRAVERS AND PRINTERS, 76 PARK PLACE, N. Y.

JOHN W. ASHBY, President.
L. K. RAWLINS, Secretary.

R. M. CLAPP, Ass't Secretary.
W. G. ROBINSON, Treasurer.

CENTRAL EXECUTIVE COMMITTEE.

THOS. F. KING.
NED E. FARRELL.

W. G. ROBINSON.

JOHN B. DELL.
G. D. WATSON.

ALACHUA COUNTY

IMMIGRATION ASSOCIATION.

OFFICE OF EXECUTIVE COMMITTEE,

GAINESVILLE, FLA.

EXECUTIVE COMMITTEE.

THOMAS F. KING, Gainesville, Fla.
W. G. ROBINSON, Gainesville, Fla.
J. A. CARLISLE, Gainesville, Fla.
JOHN W. ASHBY, Gainesville, Fla.
DR. G. D. WATSON, Windsor, Fla.
W. L. LAMBDIN, Melrose, Fla,
G. H. AMBROSE, Waldo, Fla.
C. H. FURMAN, Fairbanks, Fla.
J. J. BARR, Micanopy, Fla.
J. C. NEAL, Archer, Fla.
J. A. WILLIAMS, Newnansville, Fla.
W. F. RICE, Arredondo, Fla.
A. ZETROURER, Rochelle, Fla.
W. S. MOORE, Hawthorne, Fla.
J. CHESNUT, Jonesville, Fla.
J. B. DELL, Hague, Fla.
W. K. CESSNA, Gainesville, Fla.
H. G. MASON, Trenton, Fla.
R. H. HALL, Grove Park, Fla.
L. R. THOMAS, Ft. White, Fla.
A. HAGUE, Hague, Fla.
F. POLK, Franklin, Fla.
NED E. FARRELL, Waldo, Fla.
B. W. POWELL, Micanopy, Fla.

For information in regard to the County of Alachua, address the Secretary or Assistant Secretary or any member of the Executive Committee.

2

*The statements made in these following pages in regard to the
resources and capabilities of the County of Alachua, are vouched for
by the undersigned, with whose compliments this book is sent.*

INTRODUCTION.

In the preparation of the following pages I have endeavored to make a
plain, unvarnished statement of facts in regard to the resources and capabilities of the County of Alachua. No effort has been made to draw a fancy
sketch, or to indulge in rhetorical flourishes or poetic description, the desire
has been to tell "the truth, the whole truth and nothing but the truth," with
the assurance that a "cloud of witnesses" of unimpeachable character exist
who will vouch for the correctness of every statement made.

I regret that professional engagements have precluded me from devoting
as much time as I would have liked to the work. During its preparation the
Fall terms of the Circuit Courts have been in session, demanding the greater
part of my time.

The liberty has been taken of copying many paragraphs from the "Eden
of the South,' the trade editions of the *Alachua Advocate* and other similar
publications, in fact my labors have been those of Editor and Compiler.'

As neither the Association under whose auspices this pamphlet has been
prepared nor myself has the slightest pecuniary personal interest therein,
no motive can exist for presenting other than a truthful sketch. If after
reading the following pages many may be induced to come to "the Land of
Flowers" and make happy and prosperous homes in Alachua County, where
they will be cordially received, we shall feel amply compensated for our
labor.   J. W. ASHBY.

GAINESVILLE, FLA., January, 1888.

ALACHUA COUNTY COURT HOUSE, GAINESVILLE, FLA.

FLORIDA.

Although it has been moie than three hundred years since that portion of the new world known as Florida was first settled by civilized man, until within a comparatively recent period it has been almost an unknown country even to the American people, but during the past two decades the State has made rapid progress in wealth and population, "She is no longer unknown," but in all the elements requisite and necessary for the establishment of happy and prosperous homes, she stands to-day the peer of any country on earth.

The State is the largest east of the Mississippi river, having an area of 59,268 square miles. Of this the coast waters, bays, gulfs, sounds and harbors are put down at 1,800 square miles, rivers and smaller streams at 390, and lakes and ponds at 2,250, making the whole water surface 4,440 square miles, leaving 54,828 square miles of land surface.

Florida is principally a peninsula, shaped very much like the " boot of Italy," to which it is often and aptly compared by writers. Bounded by the Gulf of Mexico on the South and West, and the Atlantic Ocean on the East, the wonderful Gulf stream pours its mysterious volumes of heated water along its reefs and shores, equalizing in a wonderful degree the temperature of the breezes blowing across it. The State lies nearer the equator than any other portion of the United States or than the most Southerly part of Europe; is on the same parallels of latitude as the great desert of Sahara in Africa, and the most populous portions of Persia and India.

The equable temperature of Florida is one of the great excellencies of the climate. The thermometer rarely falls below 30 or 40 degrees, or rises above 96. The climate of the State is of course varied, as it extends through six degrees of latitude. The greatest heats in summer are not equal to those experienced in New York and Boston. One writer, who is considered good authority, says that during his eighteen years of residence in Florida, the greatest heat was 96 degrees in the shade. The whole State, from October till June has been characterized as one continuous spring! The nights, whatever the character of the days preceding them are cool and refreshing. Both the winter and summer weather are delightful. The medical statistics of the Army show that the climate of the State as a whole, ranks pre-eminent in point of salubrity.

The atmosphere of Florida is a medicine that has cured thousands of patients. For consumption and all pulmonary diseases whatever, for nervous disorders and for the aged, whose vital forces begin to shrink before the austerities of Northern weather, the climate of Florida is a fountain of healing and new life.

Scattered all over Florida are men and women, healthy and vigorous, who, in years gone by, came to Florida as a last resource from death. There are many others, active business men some of them, who though well and strong, yet recognize the fact that their lease of life is a contingent one, depending simply upon their remaining in Florida. They dare not return to their old homes, where the enemy still lies in wait for them.

The advice of Horace Greely to young men to "go west and grow up with the country," was appropriate when uttered, but circumstances have since brought about a changed condition of affairs. The broad prairies of the west were then holding in their fertile soil rich harvests for the laborer. And the rapidly flowing tide of immigration furnished ample and remunerative markets for all they could produce. Now the order of things is changed. To-day there are large possibilities for young men, and older ones too, in Florida. The lands may be less productive than those in the west, but they respond cordially to kind treatment, and are cheaper. In no portion of the South are there better opportunities for men than in Florida. With even small means, energy and economy, investments may be made which, with proper attention, will in a few years become very profitable.

The following article is taken from an editorial in the New Orleans *Times-Democrat* for 1886 :—

"The State of Forida is boasting of the great progress it has made in every branch of industry, in wealth, population, etc., since the census; and it has good grounds for its boasts. Its progress in six years has been as rapid as any portion of the Union and challenges comparison with the most prosperous States of the Northwest, while its educational advancement has been such as to show that it goes forward mentally and materially at the same time.

"Take the population of the State, for instance. It was 269,493 in 1880 and 342,451 in 1885, an increase of 28 per cent. This rate of increase will bring the total population of the State up to 438,337 by the next census year.

"The advance in wealth, however, has been greater than in population, the assessment of the State being $70,667,458 to-day, against $31,157,846, an increase of 127 per cent., more than doubling in six years. No other State in the Union has done as well as this in the midst of business depression. The showing is as good relatively as in the aggregate, the valuation per capita being $115.50 in 1880 and $206.63 in 1886. In this short period the average assessed wealth of every man and woman in Florida has almost doubled.

"Coming to the railroads we see the same improvement keeping march with the advance of the State. In 1880, Florida had but 528 miles; to-day she has 1,688, an increase of 1,160 or 218 per cent.

"The number of public schools in 1880 was 1,131, with an attendance of 39,315, against 1,724 to-day, with 62,327 in attendance.

"The bonded debt of the State is $1,067,400, the greater portion of which is held to the account of various educational and charitable funds, leaving only $472,700 held by outsiders, which sum is steadily diminishing. The State bonds are in demand at $1.12 to $1.25.

"Recapitulating, it is found that Florida has advanced—

"In population,	. . . . .	28 per cent.
"In assessed wealth, .		. 127 per cent.
"In railroad mileage,		218 per cent.
"In schools, . .		. 44 per cent.
"In school attendance,	. . . .	54 per cent.

"This is as good a showing as any State in the Union can make, and full of promise for the future. It is not to be wondered at that lands should be in demand in Florida, and that immigration should be pouring into the State from all parts of the Union."

The Constitution of the State of Florida provides for a liberal homestead exemption, the clause relating thereto being as follows:—

"A homestead to the extent of one hundred and sixty acres of land, or the half of one acre within the limits of an incorporated city or town, owned by the head of a family residing in this State, together with one thousand dollars worth of personal property. And the improvements on the real estate shall be exempt from forced sale under process of any Court. And the real estate shall not be liable without the joint consent of husband and wife, when that relation exists. But no property shall be exempt from sale for taxes or assessments, or for the payment of obligations contracted for the purchase of said property, or for the erection or repair of improvements on the real estate exempted, or for house, field or other labor performed on the same. The exemption herein provided for in a city or town shall not extend to more improvements or buildings than the residence and business house of the owner; and no judgment or decree or execution shall be a lien upon exempted property except as provided in this article."

This exemption inures to the widow and heirs of the party entitled thereto, and applies to all debts except those specified in the preceding paragraph.

The following article has been contributed by the Rev. George D. Watson, of Windsor, Florida:—

7

FLORIDA AND SOUTHERN CALIFORNIA COMPARED.

Having traveled through Southern California quite extensively, and also very largely through the State of Florida, it may not be out of place to state as briefly as possible a few points of honest comparison between the two localities.

Nothing is to be gained by bearing false witness against either persons or localities. Some few persons in Florida have made very ignorant and 'foolish statements about California, while land agents and newspapers in California have published the grossest slanders and falsehoods about Florida. In some things each State has superior advantages over the other. Strictly speaking, Florida is the Japan, while Southern California is the Spain of the United States. But to specify a few comparisons :—

1.—In South California there are no forests ; the whole landscape is open to view, and all the improvements put upon the soil in the way of buildings, gardens and fruit trees show to the very best advantage. In Florida there are great forests which conceal from the eye of the traveller most of the choicest improvements in the State. If the vast improvements in Florida could be laid out in unobstructed vision it would be an astonishment to the beholder.

2.—While California is a very large country, the great part of the southern portion is an uninhabitable desert. The improvable portion is a narrow strip ; hence the improvements are more compact and intensified, while in Florida the improvable property extends over a vast tract, and the towns, orchards and farms are scattered here and there over hundreds of miles in extent, and do not present that concentrated form which they do in some other sections.

3.—The temperature of Southern California is less variable than in Florida. In the latter State it has more flexibility, owing to the frequency of rains, though it has no extremes of temperature.

4.—In Southern California you buy the water; in Florida you buy the fertilizer, with this difference, however, that the water supply of Southern California is absolutely limited, and beyond a certain population it will be impossible to supply the demand, while the manure supply of Florida is utterly inexhaustible in the shape of muck and peat beds, which more and more are being used as the natural fertilizer of that soil.

5.—The nights in Southern California are deleterious, and people there will warn you against being out at night, because at night the air comes down from the snow-capped mountains, and nothing is more trying to throat and lungs than the air of melted snow. In Florida the splendor of the day is not decreased by the dangerous nights. Most of the nights in Florida are exceedingly lovely, and healthy as well.

6.—Owing to the absence of forests, lumber is very costly in Southern California, while for the opposite reason it is very cheap in Florida, so that it costs two or three times as much to build in the former as in the latter State.

7.—Many will refer to the vast amount of waste land in Florida in the shape of swamps, everglades, sand-tracts, etc. But Southern California has

8

EAST FLORIDA SEMINARY, GAINESVILLE, FLA.

a far greater waste in its rainless Mojave Desert. Southern California would gladly give millions of wealth for a few of the little lakes, tens of thousands of which begerm the territory of Florida.

8.—John Milton wrote in Paradise Lost of the stars that "shed male and female light." Many critics thought this a whimsical idea, but scientific analysis has proved his poetry to be sober fact. The same remark may be extended to cilmates. The climate of Southern California is masculine, while that of Florida is feminine. The climate of Southern California will benefit the male sex more readily, while that of Florida acts more speedily upon females. Perhaps rheumatics may find relief in California, while the climate in Florida s nearly an infallible specific for catarrh and bronchitis, while many rhuematics find entire relief in Florida, and many afflicted with catarrh find relief in California.

9.—Fuel is scarce in Southern California; the mountain sides are searched for roots for fuel, and one of the pursuits there is to grow timber for fire-wood, while in Florida it is so abundant that it costs little more than the cutting and hauling.

10.—Southern California is superior for all variety of grapes and nuts, while Florida is far superior for all citrus fruits, and all fruits grown in Japan find their natural home in Florida.

11.—Southern California is the land for the rich and luxurious classes who can spend thousands in boring artesian wells or tunneling the mountains for water supply. Property is very high there, and the laboring classes can very rarely buy themselves a home. Florida, while it possesses unlimited capabilities for the use of wealth, is emphatically the land for the poor, and no laboring man in the State need go one month without owning a few acres sufficient for a home and orchard. I have never heard of a pauper in Florida. In Alachua County, one of the richest in the State, we have no poor-house and no one living on public charity.

12.—Southern California is a great wine country, which is a serious hinderance to its moral development. Florida is largely a temperance State and a great many of its counties prohibit the sale of intoxicants. Among such counties is Alachua, the central county of the State.

13.—California is far removed from the great market of its products, while Florida is within twenty-four hours' ride of the metropolis of the Western Hemisphere and the great cities, with their aggregate millions of population

ALACHUA COUNTY.

Alachua County lies just south of the 30th degree of north latitude and between the 82 and 83 degrees of longitude west from Greenwich, is bounded on the north by Suwannee, Columbia and Bradford Counties; east, by the Counties of Clay and Putnam; south by Marion and Levy, and west by

"BARRACKS," EAST FLORIDA SEMINARY, GAINESVILLE, FLA.

Lafayette, from which it is separated by the Suwannee River. Its population by the census of June, 1885, was 26,255, a gain of 9,793 over census of 1880. A larger increase and a larger population than any other County in the State. It has an area of 1,260 square miles or 806,400 acres.

The County is 250 feet above the ocean's level, far enough South to be free from the ice and snow and chilling winds of the North, fanned by the gentle breezes which come wafted from the Gulf of Mexico and the Atlantic Ocean, the distance to either being about forty-five miles. Although not below the mythical frost line, the winters are neither cold nor freezing, but generally cool and bracing, cloudy and disagreeable days being the exception, fair and sunny ones being the rule, the summer being of longer duration but the heat not so oppressive as midsummer at the North. For natural beauties, fertility of soil, perfect drainage, a light, dry and invigorating atmosphere, good water, good society, healthfulness and educational advantages the County is not excelled by any portion of the State of Florida.

The great natural fertility and beauty of this section of the State is historical. In the latter days of Spanish dominion in Florida, Fernando de la Maza Arredondo, a wealthy merchant of Havana, had established throughout the eastern part of the province, numerous trading posts, where the untutored savage exchanged his splendidly tanned buckskins for the fanciful devices and seductive *wi-ho-me* (fire-water) of the pale-faces. His goods were bartered in the remotest villages of the red man, and the barges of his agents and factors found out the secret ways of the hundred creeks that flow into the St. Johns river.

To these men the Indians imparted the information of a country in the interior, filled with grand forests, high-rolling hills, broad prairies, beautiful lakes and abundant streams whose united currents poured themselves into a wonderful chasm in the earth. *A-la-chu-a*, these red men called it, meaning big-jug, a jug without a bottom ; it is from this that the County takes its name, now pronounced Ah-lach-u-a.

With admirable enterprise and splendid courage Dexter and Wanton, the Saxon agents of the Spanish Arredondo, penetrated to this country and established near the wonderful " big-jug " their trading-post. Land was free in those days. One had only to find where the good lands were and he found little trouble in getting a royal patent. Being impressed with the beauty and fertility of this section, Arredondo & Son obtained a Spanish grant for about 289,645 English acres of land within the territory now known as the County of Alachua.

Alachua County is believed to be as healthy as any part of the United States. Fatal bilious fever is rare, except under great exposure to the malaria of low hammocks, rivers, etc., chills and fever are not frequent and are of the mildest and most easily managed types. Physicians all testify that diseases are less stubborn in Florida and less liable to terminate in death than the same kind of disease in higher latitudes. For a territory so large the death rate is exceedingly small. The pine lands, which are unusually healthy, are

12

nearly everywhere studded at intervals of a few miles with rich hammock land varying in extent from twenty to forty thousand acres. Residences only half a mile from cultivated hammocks in any part of Florida are notably free from malarial diseases, while residences on even the high hammock lands in Alachua County are generally found to be healthy.

"Carl" Webber, in his excellent work, entitled "The Eden of the South" divides the lands of Alachua County into six classes, as follows: First, second and third class, pine lands, high and low hammock lands and swamp lands. The fertility and durability of even third class pine lands has been amply proven, and it has been established that pine swampy lands are not without great value. That which appears to consist of a white sand soil on third-class pine land is not all sand, which is seen by the eye. There is a mixture of fine comminuted bits of shells, or carbonate of lime, which furnishes the plants of such region with an important element of plant food. All second-class pine lands are productive. Underlying the surface is clay, marl, lime rock and sand. These lands are easily accessible, productive, cheaply fertilized by cattle, and, by reason of their supposed healthfulness above hammock lands, are most readily settled upon. The fertility of first-class pine lands is indeed wonderful, while the limit of their durability is still unknown. The surface for several inches is covered with a dark vegetable mold, beneath which to a depth of several feet is a chocolate sand loam, mixed for the most part with limestone pebbles, and resting on a sub-stratum of marl, clay or limestone. The hammock lands are the most productive. Both the high and the low hammocks are generally admixed with lime, and the streams running through them are impregnated with it more or less. High hammock do not require ditching or draining. Low hammock generally require ditching to relieve them of a superabundance of water, especially during the rainy season. They have a deeper soil and are generally regarded as more lasting than high hammocks. Low hammocks are especially fitted for the growth of sugar-cane, as are also the swamp lands, which are held to be the most durable rich lands in Florida. In Alachua County hammock lands predominate, more especially in the belt of land running through the center of the county from the northwest to the southeast portion. The open hammock lands are hilly and pebbly; the soil is a dark loam, underlaid with a chocolate colored, friable clay. On the high mixed pine and hammock lands most of the oldest, largest and most productive plantations are situated, although some of the old planters preferred the first-class pine land for general cropping, using for fertilizers cotton seed and pea-vines, by which means annual products were generally insured.

There are in Alachua County, like all places of mixed people, representatives of nearly every sect in the Christian religion, and in the larger places a goodly sprinkling of Jews. The churches, however, are principally Baptist, Episcopalian, Methodist and Presbyterian, all of which are well supported and presided over by able preachers.

The white people of Alachua represent every State in the Union, from Maine

13

to California, and are in their moral and intellectual status, of the advanced classes from the old States. Intelligence predominates in all the essential avenues of business, and in the principal occupations of life. The colored people have caught the spirit of advanced enlightenment and enterprise which prevails, and show remarkable traits of character, keeping up their churches, and being good citizens. There are to a slight degree distinct classes of society the same as found elsewhere, but there is no ostracism of settlers from other places, as the county is now largely composed of people who, within the past twenty years, have themselves settled here from other States. The future growth and prosperity depend upon an increase of such settlers, who bring, with new ideas, a new spirit of improvement and increased wealth. All worthy new comers are heartily welcomed and will meet with well wishes on every hand. The only division of the people is political, the same as elsewhere, but the same candid expression and the same freedom of speech is allowable here as in New England.

Any man can succeed in this county by industry, economy, and application to business. Whatever subsistence he needs he can produce at home, and while doing this, he can care for his orange grove, orchard and vineyard. With a small sum of money, enough to purchase his land, clear and fence, put up his buildings and tide him over the first year without contracting debt, his rapid prosperity will be assured. There are thousands of people in the over crowded cities of the North now eking out a miserable existence whose interests might be promoted by coming to Florida. To those who have only a few hundred dollars to commence with, and who are not afraid to work this county affords an inviting field. Every man, no matter how poor, if economical and industrious can secure for himself a home in Alachua County. While this is the case now, it is reasonably certain that in a few years the price of real estate will place it beyond the reach of those who need homes most. Every transfer made enhances the value of real estate in this county, and will continue. No better opportunity will ever occur than is now offered for the procurement of a home.

In winter Alachua County is a sanitarium for invalids and a resort for sportsmen and pleasure-seekers. The air is dry, light and invigorating. The natural water sheds preserve the rainfall from standing and stagnating, or the sandy soil absorbs it like a sponge, and it is carried off by natural under drains. All over the county there are numbers of large bearing orange trees that have never have been materially injured by cold. Facts show that counties situated south of Alachua have no practical advantage over this county in the successful cultivation of the orange; but this has an incalculable advantage over most of them in adaptability to general farming and accessibility to the great commercial marts of the country. There are thousands of acres of valuable lands on the market, which can now be purchased at reasonable prices. There is enough available land to enable the settler to select a home where he and his family would enjoy health, and may surround himself with groves, orchards, vegetables and abundant field crops.

14

Those who simply pass through on the railroads see but little of what Alachua County really is. The roads have been built along the lowlands mainly, where tracklaying was easy, and only glimpses are afforded of hills and valleys beyond. One can readily understand why the tourist, who views the country from the window of a Pullman, should report Florida a land of sand, but take a team and drive throughout the county and the scene changes. If one could get a birds-eye view of many sections, the land would appear like an ocean of forest and farm, rolling in billows. North and west of Gainesville,

H. F. DUTTON'S RESIDENCE, GAINESVILLE.

the country is undulating, containing many hills and valleys. The fertility of the soil of Alachua was well-known in ante-bellum days, as the sad remains of many an old plantation testify.

Here "Befo' de wah" many a Florida magnate, surrounded by his dusky retainers, ruled his wide domain, dispensing hospitality with a lavish hand and living and dying in peace and plenty. Only a few of them remain, no longer magnates, but prosperous planters still.

The soil of Alachua County is admirably adapted to general farming. All the cereals do well. Tobacco from Havana seed has been cultivated with

15

success. Oranges, peaches, pears, plums, grapes, strawberries, figs, melons and vegetables of every kind grow luxuriantly. By using improved methods of cultivation an abundant support for a family can be obtained from five acres of land, in growing early fruits and vegetables for the Eastern markets. It has been often said that cattle raising and dairy farming cannot be profitably conducted in Florida. The statement is certainly untrue, as far as Alachua County is concerned; many of the planters have fine blooded stock and plenty of them, with an abundance of milk and butter.

NATURAL CURIOSITIES OF ALACHUA.

The magnificent lakes and many natural curiosities of Alachua County deserve special mention.

ALACHUA LAKE, about one and one half miles south of Gainesville, the county seat, is now a beautiful sheet of water coveringa large area. Not many years ago it was a large and beautiful prairie, known as Payne's prairie. It took its name from King Payne, an old Seminole chief of an early day. This prairie was a great grazing ground for the Indians' cattle, and in later years, was devoted to a like purpose and for tillage by the whites. In those days thousands of cattle and sheep could be seen at any time enjoying the richness which mother earth supplies. The overflow of Newnans lake, which lies to the north of it, formed a stream which wended its way through the prairie and emptied itself into one of the curiosities of the State known as the Sink. There the waters found their way into some subterraneous passage whose mystery has not yet been solved. Some years ago this sink became clogged and the waters were forced to remain upon the surface, and overflowed the prairie, covering roads, cultivated fields and grazing grounds, creating an additional lake in the county, which is now one of its natural curiosities. The locality where the waters became clogged is still known as "the Sink," and is one of the most romantic picnic grounds and pleasure resorts in the State. About this prairie and among the lakes in this region, was the Indians' favorite fishing and hunting ground when they inhabited this part of the State.

TUSCAWILLA LAKE, about one mile square, is situated near the town of Micanopy, and was named for the daughter of the Indian Chief for whom the town was named. This lake, like Alachua lake, was created by the clogging of a sink, with the following differences. The sink was smaller, so that in rainy weather a lake was created which would gradually disappear in a dry season. Desiring to prevent a temporary clogging of this sink the owner of the property some years ago endeavored to open this cavern and keep it open by log barriers. During the operation his logs caved in and the sink became permanently clogged, and the lake consequently permanently located.

SANTA FE LAKE is a delightful body of water, and can boast of many fine residences upon its borders, as well as many magnificent orange groves. It is about nine miles long and four miles wide at its widest points.

LAKE ALTO is about one mile east of Waldo. It is about one mile and a half long by one mile wide. Santa Fe and Alto Lakes are the highest bodies of water in the County. Situated upon a high ridge or back of the peninsula, they have outlets extending both east and west to the Atlantic Ocean and the Gulf.

NEWNANS LAKE. five miles east of Gainesville, and between Santa Fe and Alachua lakes, is one of the prettiest bodies of water in the State. It is about six miles long by two and a half miles wide, has a good sandy bed and is surrounded by beautiful groves and rich hammock lands.

Levey, Ledworth, Wauberg, and many other beautiful lakes are to be found in different sections of the County.

H. F. DUTTON & CO.'S COTTON GIN, GAINESVILLE

All the lakes named abound with different varieties of fish. Such is the mildness of the winters that they increase more rapidly than in colder latitudes and are caught at all seasons of the year. Among the varieties are the trout (black bass of the North), sucker, mud or black fish, bream, perch and pike. Many of these are not excelled, if equaled, in size, flavor, or number in any part of the South. The trout is the largest, having been caught weighing twenty-five pounds. Its flesh is white, firm and delightful to the taste. Great quantities of fish have been caught in those lakes in seines, and shipped to other states, but this is now prohibited by law, and in consequence they will multiply vastly and become inexhaustible.

DEVIL'S MILL HOPPER. About five miles north of Gainesville, over a pleasant road, is one of nature's grandest curiosities, called "The Devil's Mill

Hopper," covering about three acres on top, one hundred and fifty feet deep, with sides sloping like a bowl, which are green with running vines, while ferns of different varieties, some of which are not to be found in any other part of the State, carpet the banks with their grateful foliage. Magnolias of large size, the thrifty live oak and its companion the water oak, and numerous varities of trees of hard wood, make a home for birds of bright plumage, and the mocking bird makes his presence known by his sweet song. Descending by an easy incline through the foliage, one stands amazed at this wonderful freak of nature, and wonders if some magic charm has not been thrown around•him and opened the gate to some fairy scene or enchanted place. Numerous streams, some fifteen in number, starting from out the sides, looking like ribbons of silver, disappear, and again come out from their background of green, tumbling over the phosphate rocks, making cascades and pools and forming at the bottom of the hopper a small lake from which there is no visible outlet; and although the streams have been continuously pouring down the mossy and fern clad bank beyond the memory of man, the little lake, with its finny inhabitants, undisturbed by the elements which formed it, does not raise or lower its surface, but keeps its level and goes where no man knows.

NATURAL WELLS are most frequently found in the western part of the county, and are great wonders. These wells are as round and as perpendicular as if they had been cut through the rock by the hand of man. The most of these contain water, but some of them are dry. In diameter they are about two and a half feet, and are from thirty to forty feet deep. The walls are of solid limestone. The water in them contains lime, and in summer is quite cool. The dry wells are perfectly safe to enter. In one, at least, parties can go down in it a distance of thirty feet, and then through an underground passage can come up out of another one, one mile away.

SCHOOLS.

The public school system of Florida was inaugurated by the State Constitution of 1868, and has steadily grown in favor and usefulness. Schools have been established in every neighborhoood, are provided with efficient teachers and are well attended. In addition to the public schools quite a number of private schools exist which are well patronized.

EAST FLORIDA SEMINARY,

Located at Gainesville, the county seat, is a State school with an endowment derived from the sale of lands donated to Florida by the general government. It is controlled by a Board of Education whose members are appointed by the Governor. By authority of the laws of Florida, the school is organized upon a collegiate and military plan and is authorized to grant diplomas and confer degrees.

The academic building, erected by the citizens of Gainesville, is handsome and commodious and furnished with the best educational appliances.

The Dormitory or "Barracks," erected by the State of Florida, is an imposing wooden structure, with rooms for the residence of instructors and cadets, and all necessary attachments of infirmary, mess hall, kitchen, etc. Teachers and cadets live in this building and take their meals together in the mess hall. The cadets are thus at all times under the immediate supervision and control of the instructors and officers of the school.

The academic department of the seminary is so organized as to prepare students for admission into the higher classes of colleges and universities, or to fit them for immediate entrance into the practical duties of life. The *eleves* of the school are now filling positions of trust and usefulness in all portions of the State.

The military system is modeled after that of West Point, and has been for the past five years under the control of an officer of the United States Army detailed by the Secretary of War for duty at this school.

Cadets from Northern and Northwestern States, unable to attend school in their own sections on account of predisposition to disease, have found at the East Florida Seminary a combination of climatic conditions and of educational work and military regime exactly suited to their constitutional needs; and coming to the school as invalids they have invariably returned to their homes in the enjoyment of robust health.

The seminary numbers among its students representatives from nearly all the counties of Florida east of the Suwannee river (its legal territory) and also from other States, and it is beyond question the most prosperous, successful and efficient school in Florida.

UNION ACADEMY, a school for the education of colored people, is the largest in Alachua County. This school was organized under the auspices of the Freedman's Bureau in 1866. The school, therefore, is in its twenty-second year. After being under its direction for some time, its management was transferred to the County Board of Education. The methods, classification and branches taught were such as are found in the country schools and ordinary town schools. This school has been thoroughly graded, and consists of Primary, Intermediate and Normal departments. It is located at Gainesville.

TRANSPORTATION FACILITIES.

Next to the fertility of soil, purity of water and healthfulness. and the advanced social, educational and moral conditions of Alachua County, the facilities for transportation and travel are chief inducements to immigration. These, of late, have been greatly increased to meet the demand of growing population, agriculture and trade. The Florida Railway and Navigation Company's Railroad, from Fernandina to Cedar Key, uniting the Atlantic and Gulf of Mexico, runs nearly east and west not far from the center of the county. Gainesville, and all the towns and villages along its route have rapidly improved since the construction of this road, to afford convenient centers of trade to surrounding neighborhoods as they have grown in numbers and prospered in agricultural pursuits. From Waldo a branch of the F. R. & N. runs south on the east side of Orange Lake to Ocala, Marion County, through an inviting section of Alachua County, which is being rapidly settled. From Gainesville, the county site, the Florida Southern Railway runs east, with the terminus at Palatka, on the St. Johns river. The Florida Southern crosses a branch of the F. R. & N. at Hawthorne, in this county, twenty-two miles east of Gainesville. Nearly midway between these two places, at Rochelle, the main trunk of the Florida Southern runs south, along the west side of Orange Lake, celebrated for its immense orange groves, budded on the forest of wild trees, and the production of enormous crops of vegetables. The Savannah, Florida and Western Railway is thoroughly equipped, affording ample and first-class accommodations for the transportation of passengers and freight to all points North and Northwest.

The Georgia Southern and Florida Railway, which is now being constructed from Macon, Georgia, to Palatka, Florida, will pass through the eastern portion of the county. The officers of the Gainesville, Tallahassee and Western

CORN AND COTTON FIELDS.

Railway Company express great confidence in being able to construct this road at an early day. This road, which would pass through the western portion of the county, would develop a fine timber and agricultural region, and would greatly advance the material interests of the whole county. Charters are held for railroads from Gainesville to Rocky Point, in this county, and also from Gainesville to Windsor, on Lake Newnan, in this county. All these roads will be constructed in due course of time. Alachua Lake, Lake Newnan, Lochloosa Lake and Orange Lake, are all navigable, affording ample facilities for the transportation of the orange and vegetable crops produced around their borders. The Santa Fe river has a deep, navigable channel from Fort White to its entrance into the Suwannee, and the latter river, which is the western boundary of this county, is navigable for steamers from Cedar Key, on the Gulf. The Santa Fe canal, with the lakes connected thereby, gives transportation facilities from Waldo to Melrose and along the route. It can readily be seen, therefore, that Alachua is not second to any county in the State in the number, convenience and excellence of inland rail and water ways for public use.

PRODUCTS OF ALACHUA.

No county in the State of Florida, nor elsewhere, it is confidently believed, can boast of a greater variety of products than the County of Alachua. Wheat is the only cereal that cannot be abundantly produced; corn, oats and vegetables can be raised in the greatest profusion for home consumption. So can stock of all kinds be reared in as great numbers as necessity may demand. Corn for meal, and hominy, oats, rice, sugar, syrup, tobacco and vegetables can be produced in larger quantities on any good or fertilized land than may be required for home use, and the excess can readily be sold for good prices. From this revenue the farmer can supply himself and family with flour, coffee and many luxuries. Potatoes, chufas, pinders, pumpkins, etc., will fatten all the hogs necessary for meat. Any farmer in Alachua, if he will be industrious, can make his occupation self-sustaining and independent of the fatal system of credit. He can easily produce all the bread, meat, sugar and syrup needful for his family and employees, and all the provender for his work-animals on his own land. Then he will be prepared to draw all the ready money he can out of fruits, vegetables and cotton, supplemented by sale of butter, eggs, poultry, lard. stock, etc. He will be enabled to improve his surroundings, purchase whatever else he may require, and live as independently as a lord.

Vegetable raising is an industry which in Alachua County has grown to wonderful proportions within a few years, paying large profits of several hundreds of dollars per acre on crops that fortunately ripen and reach the markets at the right moment. This County will undoubtedly produce not only the greatest variety of marketable and profitable crops of any region in the State, and is unexcelled by any State in the Union. And yet a large proportion of the visitors to the State go up and down the St. Johns river without dreaming of the productiveness of this region.

The vegetables which can be profitably cultivated in Alachua County may be enumerated as follows: Artichokes, beans, beets, cabbages, celery, cucumbers, egg plant, Irish potatoes, lettuce, okra, onions, parsnips, peas, pumpkins, radishes, squashes, sweet potatoes, tomatoes, turnips.

CABBAGES form one of the staple crops for export to the Northern markets. In the early vegetable line they stand first in importance. The acreage is every year increasing, in consequence of the certainty of both crop and profits. The yield is from one hundred to one hundred and fifty barrels per acre, and the price realized is from three to five dollars per barrel.

CUCUMBERS have paid largely to the early grower and are esteemed as a profitable crop, the price realized being an average of two dollars a crate.

IRISH POTATOES have taken a very prominent place among the profitable early crops in Florida. On the best class of land about thirty barrels of first-class shipping potatoes per acre are raised, which, getting into the Eastern markets about the time the old crop is exhausted, have been netting over cost of shipping and selling, about four dollars per barrel. These figures have been very much exceeded in many localities.

SWEET POTATOES come nearer being a universal crop in Florida than any other the soil produces. They are easily propagated from the roots, sprouts or vines, and sometimes the seed, though the latter mode is rarely used. From its easy propagation and cultivation, its large yield and the variety and excellence of the dishes prepared from it, it is one of the indispensable crops.

BEETS, BEANS, EGG-PLANT, TOMATOES, and very many other vegetables, are all profitable crops and grown in very large quantities for shipment to the Northern markets.

Those who have never investigated the subject can form no adequate idea of the amount raised or of the profitableness of vegetable culture in the State of Florida. Many persons are not only making money but are rapidly becoming rich from raising vegetables for the Northern markets.

The importance of market gardening to the State is almost incalculable. It was first started but comparatively a few years ago as an experiment, but has become a leading industry. Orange groves may be planted on the same land with vegetables, thus securing for a man of small means a future period of independence and enjoyment, while present needs are being provided for. It is an industry which is attracting to the State a class of immigrants whose intelligence and industry is rapidly converting the great wilderness heretofore existing into most valuable estates, adding greatly to the growth, prosperity and power of the State.

No section of the State of Florida offers such great advantages for vegetable growing as the County of Alachua, and no other county in the State is engaged so extensively in the business. Alachua may properly be denominated the garden County of Florida.

Other products of the soil, which have not been referred to, and which may be cultivated with profit, are as follows : –Arrow-root, barley, castor-beans, cassava, chufas, coontie, corn, cotton, fiber plants, grass, goobers, melons, millet, oats, pinders, rice, rye, sorghum, sugar-cane, tobacco and wheat.

CASTOR-BEANS can be as successfully raised in Alachua County as in any country in the world. They are always in demand, and command good prices.

The farmers of Alachua can produce castor-beans on their poorest lands and realize handsome returns in cash. There is no substantial reason why their production could not be made at once one of the chief industries of the farmers of the county. There is no doubt of the fact that castor-beans can be produced in enormous quantities, and there seems no doubt of the further fact that a ready market could be found at remunerative prices. Those who engage in this enterprise first will in all probability be well paid for their trouble.

CORN is easily and cheaply made and is of superior quality, both for bread and stock. Alachua County could produce all the corn needed for the

IN THE CANE PATCH.

entire peninsula of Florida. Sixty bushels per acre has often been raised, but soil, cultivation, season and manure make a very wide difference in the individual yields. Fifteen bushels will be a fair average of the actual crop. The cultivation of corn would be very profitable, if the same effort was made as is done with other crops. Formerly, no corn was shipped into this county; but as other crops, which bring ten times as much per acre, give money to pay for corn, many persons do not plant it except for table use. Two crops of corn can be grown on the same land in one year. A variety of early corn is planted in February or early in March, which ripens by the middle or end of May, if seasons are favorable.

COTTON.—The long cotton of Florida has come to rank in fineness and quality with the cotton grown on the Sea Islands of South Carolina and Georgia, which States for a hundred years have grown the finest produced in the world. There is no country so well adapted to the growth of this particular staple as Florida, and the numerous growers of cotton all over Alachua County have shown themselves adepts in its culture. It will not grow on the uplands of Georgia and South Carolina without losing its distinctive quality and becoming short and coarse. The peculiar geographical position of Florida, lying, as it does, between the Atlantic and Gulf, its shores washed by the Gulf Stream, produces an atmosphere adapted to the improvement of the length, strength and fineness of the staple nowhere else to be found. Hence Florida, by nature, is favored above all other countries for producing this beautiful staple, that is spun into hand and sewing-machine thread, from No. 8 to No. 500, into most beautiful laces, wherewith ladies add to the taste and elegance of their dress, and so deftly mixed and woven into the finest silks, satins and fine velvets, that it is impossible to tell, and only the best detectives can detect it. Lovely women, with elaborate and costly-made silk dresses, do not know that much of the material is Florida long cotton, which makes the silk a better article and makes it wear and last longer and, to all appearance, is as pretty, as good and elegant as the best from the looms of Lyons, France. Two hundred pounds of lint-cotton per acre has been grown, but about one hundred pounds would be an average crop without fertilizing. The price varies from eighteen to thirty-five cents per pound.

OATS is a reliable and important crop, yielding on good average soil, properly prepared, from fifteen to forty bushels per acre.

RICE is a crop that is common, but not grown in the county on as large a scale as its value would justify. The variety known as upland rice is best, and yields from twenty to one hundred bushels per acre. The lack of facilities for cleaning has hitherto held this crop in check, but the introduction of rice machinery has given to it a new impetus, and in future a much larger crop than ever before will be raised.

SORGHUM does not form a staple crop, although it offers many points that, if utilized, would pay well. One reason for this is, that it has been regarded as a competitor of the sugar-cane; in this it does certainly fail. Sorghum can not compete with tropical cane, if sugar is to be the sole product, but sorghum has been raised with paying success on its own merits, and offers, as a syrup-producing plant, the possibility of having new syrup at a time when tropical cane is still green. In addition to this, two crops a year have been raised, one planted in April and cut in July, and another planted in July and cut in October, both yielding syrup, seed and fodder, the seed being of itself equal to an ordinary crop of corn from the same land.

SUGAR-CANE is a regular crop, every farmer having his patch varying in size from one-half to three or four acres. Sugar is not generally made, as syrup from Florida cane is of superior quality and commands a good price. From ten to twenty barrels of syrup may be produced from one acre.

TOBACCO has for many years been raised on a small scale, but the recent introduction of fine seed has demonstrated that in Alachua County can be raised a tobacco equal to the far-famed Cuba cigar leaf. Trial crops during the past year have instructed the people, and many farmers are preparing to plant largely. It promises to pay exceedingly well where intelligent care is used.

WHEN AND WHAT TO PLANT.

Below is given briefly what may generally be adopted for this County:—

JANUARY.—Plant Irish potatoes, peas, beets, turnips, cabbage and all hardy or semi-hardy vegetables. Make hot beds for pushing the more tender plants, such as melons, tomatoes, okra, egg-plants, etc. Set out fruit and other trees and shrubbery.

FEBRUARY.—Keep planting for a succession, same as in January. Plant vines of all kinds, shrubbery and fruit trees of all kinds, especially of the citrus family, snap-beans, corn; bed sweet potatoes for draws and slips. Oats may also be still sown, as they are in previous months.

MARCH.— Corn, oats and planting of February may be continued. Transplant tomatoes, egg-plants, melons, beans and vines of all kinds. Mulberries and blackberries are now ripening.

APRIL.—Plant as in March, except Irish potatoes, kohl rabi, and turnips. Continue to transplant tomatoes, okra, egg-plants; sow millet, corn, cow-peas, for fodder; plant the butter-bean, lady peas; dig Irish potatoes, onions, beets, and usual early vegetables should be plenty for the table.

MAY.—Plant sweet potatoes for draws in beds; continue planting corn for table; snap-beans, peas and cucumbers ought to be well forward for use; continue planting okra, egg-plants, pepper and butter-beans.

25

JUNE.—The heavy planting of sweet potatoes and cow-peas is now in order; Irish potatoes, tomatoes and a great variety of table vegetables are now ready, as also plums, early peaches and grapes.

JULY.—Sweet potatoes and cow-peas are safe to plant, the rainy season being favorable; grapes, peaches and figs are in full season; orange trees may be set out if the season is wet.

AUGUST.—Finish up planting sweet potatoes and cow peas; sow cabbage, cauliflower, turnips for fall planting; plant kohl rabi, rutabagoes; transplant orange trees and bud; last of the month plant a few Irish potatoes and beans.

SEPTEMBER.—Now is the time to commence for the true winter garden, the garden which is commenced in the North in April and May. Plant the whole range of vegetables, except sweet potatoes; set out asparagus, onion sets and strawberry plants.

OCTOBER.—Plant same as last month; put in garden peas; set out strawberries and cabbage plants; dig sweet potatoes; sow oats, rye, etc.

NOVEMBER.—A good month for garden. Continue to plant and trans-

plant, same as for October; sow oats, barley and rye for winter pasturage or crops; dig sweet potatoes; house or bank them; make sugar and syrup.

DECEMBER.—Clear up generally; fence, ditch, manure and sow, and plant hardy vegetables; plant, set out orange trees, fruit trees and shrubbery. Keep a sharp look out for an occasional frost. A slight protection will prevent injury.

It will be seen from the above that there is no month in the year but what fresh and growing vegetables can be had for sale and domestic use. This latter is a large item in the expense of living. The soil is so easily worked, so easily cultivated, that most of garden work can be performed by even delicate ladies and young children of both sexes. No frozen clods to break or rocks to remove. A garden once put in condition, properly managed, will produce abundantly and constantly. The rapid growth assures large and tender vegetables and early and luscious fruits. A single season will afford strawberries

26

"WAY DOWN UPON DE S'WANNEE RIBBER."

from the setting out, ripe figs from two-year-old cuttings, grapes the second year, peaches the second and third years; oranges from the bud from three to five years. At a little cost, a little care, one can literally sit under his own vine and fig tree and enjoy fresh-plucked fruit the whole year.

HONEY.

One of the undeveloped industries of Alachua County is the honey business. All over the county wild bees abound and many a hapless colony has had its home chopped down and robbed of its sweet treasure and then left to shift for themselves. There are few things that will give as good results for capital invested, if properly applied, as this industry.

Honey is rapidly becoming a staple product of Alachua County, whose flora seems specially adapted to the propagation of bees. Even in the winter months there is a supply of flowers quite sufficient to support the hives. This permits heavier tolls to be made on them, as less honey must be left to feed during winter.

STOCK RAISING.

This in Alachua County is one of the most profitable incidents to a farm life. It is not in any instance made an exclusive business, but thousands of domestic animals are raised every year.¶

HORSES are raised on the prairies, and cost nothing for food; winter and summer they feed on a natural pasturage. The native horse is not large, but is a tough, useful, healthy and reliable animal.

CATTLE are allowed to run in the open ranges, winter feeding or protection of any kind being an exception to the rule. Remote from the town and vegetable growing region are large tracts of land which are only utilized for stock raising. There is a cash market always open for all cattle which are offered for sale.

SHEEP pay very well, as feed costs nothing and as no protection is required even in winter. It is readily seen that the wool and all increase is profit. No very large flocks are kept.

HOGS are numerous and of all varieties, from the "razor back" to pure Essex, Berkshire, &c. Alachua, in days gone by, made all her pork and bacon, and now many farmers make a full supply every year. All might readily do so.

LUMBER.

The Lumber business in Florida is conducted upon an extensive scale. Experimental test has already determined the timber from Florida to be the best upon the market and the mills and shipments are increasing by a heavy percentage. Even Mexico and Central America are being supplied with cross-ties for their railroads from Florida pine. In Alachua County large areas exist of magnificent timber. In addition to the pine there are cypress, oak, cedar, hickory, red bay and other woods which are valuable.

To the orchardist as well as the horiculturist the County of Alachua is an inviting field. The soil is peculiarly adapted to the production of fruits of almost all descriptions. The number of persons at present engaged in the industry is far less than it should be, considering the rare opportunity offered for money making by the cultivation of fruits for shipment to Northern and Western markets. This County and State should be a land of fruits, for the land and climate are adapted to them and the absence of severe cold in the winter exempts them from the hazards that attend fruit raising in the Northern States.

The fruits which may be successfully grown in Alachua County are as follows: Bananas, blackberries, blueberries, citron, figs, grapes, grape-fruit, guavas, Kelsey plum, lemons, huckleberries, Japan persimmon, Japan plum, nectarines, olives, oranges, peaches, pears, pecans, pomegranates, quince, shaddocks, strawberries and walnuts.

ORANGES can be more extensively and profitably grown in Florida than in any other State in the Union, and from the advantages which the State enjoys in certain peculiarities of climate, soil and season, it is more than likely that it will ever retain a superiority over any other section of the country in its productions. Some of the largest and most successful orange groves in the State are in Alachua. A number of wild sour groves, which are most hardy, have been transformed by budding into the sweetest of fruit, while the many young seedling groves coming into high bearing all over the county attest their power to withstand severe frosts like those of the past year or two. Experienced growers are satisfied that the cold, so much talked of and feared, is rather beneficial than otherwise to orange groves. The cold is sure death to the insects that ravage the tree, and while it causes the trees to throw off their leaves, the fruit is much better the following year.

The history of orange growing in Florida, as an industry, is comparatively recent, but the profitableness of the business has been practically demonstrated. There is no shadow of doubt as to the really sure and safe ground for the investment of untold thousands of dollars in making orange groves.

One thousand dollars per acre per annum has time and again been realized from this business. Indeed, double that amount per acre has been frequently made; and with proper culture and fertilization, where the latter is needed, $1,000 per acre may be regarded as an available crop.

An undoubted authority on orange culture in Florida says: "Orange culture will pay beyond any other agricultural pursuit, even should the price fall as low as 75 cents per box. When reduced to that price fifty millions of boxes would not over-supply the demand of the present population of the United States and Canada. There are thirty States producing apples and peaches, and yet both these crops, which have to be marketed within a few weeks or months, are grown with profit. With such facts before us, we have nothing to fear as to over-production of the orange. The excellence of the

Florida orange is now so generally known that many other oranges are sold under that name."

An unanswerable argument in favor of the immense profits to be realized from orange culture is to be found in the fact that very many persons in Florida now in the enjoyment of opulence are indebted alone for their fortunate condition to this golden fruit. Fortunes have not only been made but are yet to be made by the industrious horticulturist in the County of Alachua; but in this, as in all other vocations of life, success is to be attained only by energetic effort.

PEACH GROWING is becoming one of the most important industries of Alachua, and is destined to be one of the most profitable. With proper care and cultivation, quite a number of varieties will fruit annually and prolifically. It is the early varieties of peaches which pay best, as they may be grown so as to reach the New York market in May, where they have brought most fabulous prices. The first of these early varieties is the Pien-tau, a Chinese fruit, which ripens about the first week in May. It is a hardy and rapid grower and is a fruit of delicious flavor. This is followed by the honey peach, about three weeks later. The Florida native and other varieties of peaches do well.

PEARS have been found to succeed well. Of the varieties grown the LeConte is one of the most popular, it being a vigorous grower, attaining large size, coming early into bearing and being said to be absolutely blight proof. Very many entertain the opinion that a pear orchard will prove as profitable as an orange grove, and many acres of this delicious fruit have been and are being planted.

GRAPES, both of the native and foreign varieties, succeed well and have paid handsome profits to those engaged in their culture. It has been demonstrated that wines of the finest variety can be manufactured from grapes grown in Florida, but it is not only in the making of wine that grape culture here has been found a paying business, but grapes shipped to the Northern markets bring handsome returns.

PLUMS of several varieties are grown. Of these the variety known as Kelsey's Japan plum deserves special mention. It comes into bearing within two or three years, and in productiveness is unsurpassed. The fruit is very large in size, being from seven to nine inches in circumference, attractive in appearance, excellent in quality, melting, rich, and juicy.

JAPAN PERSIMMON has been grown to some extent and has given such general good satisfaction that it will become one of the leading fruits. The merits of this fruit are the early bearing age of the tree and its wonderful fertility, In shape and general appearance it resembles a large, smooth tomato. The flesh is soft, with a pleasant, sweet, slight apricot flavor. Some specimens are seedless.

STRAWBERRIES of the finest flavor are produced in all parts of the County. They are easily cultivated and the yield per acre is frequently as high as four thousand quarts. Within the past two or three years the devel-

A HAMMOCK HOME.

opment of this industry has been remarkable. It is believed to be within the bounds of reason to say that not less than five hundred thousand quarts of strawberries were produced in Alachua County in the season of 1887. The fruit comes into the market too early to find competition from other states, and Florida strawberries enjoy a monopoly in the eastern sea-board markets for many weeks during January, February and March. The production and shipment of the berries North has assumed such proportions as to secure the provision by the transportation companies of suitable refrigerating cars for their preservation in transit.

CITIES, TOWNS AND POST OFFICES.

ALACHUA, a station and post office, on the Savannah, Florida and Western Railroad, fifteen miles north of Gainesville, contains two Saw-Mills, two Cotton Gins, two Grist Mills, and a Shingle Machine, all in good running order, and about one dozen dwelling houses. It is the center of a first-class agricultural region.

ARREDONDO is a shipping station on the Florida Railway and Navigation Company's line, six miles south-west from Gainesville. It is settled for some miles around by farmers and vegetable growers, whose products are among the richest revenues to the County. The lands are rich and fertile, responding with alacrity to cultivation, and yielding rich returns. The soil is largely mixed with finely comminuted bits of shell or corbonate of lime, which furnishes a natural fertilizer almost exhaustless. Thousands of crates of vegetables are annually shipped from this station to the Northern markets. The population of Arredondo is about two hundred. The place has three Stores, two Churches and School buildings.

ARCHER is a business town on the Florida Railway and Navigation Company's line, near the southern line of the County. It has nine general stores, one Drug store, two Cotton Gins, two Smith shops, one Wagon shop, two white and three colored Churches, one white and two colored Schools. It is in Section 17, Township 11, South of Range 18, East, on the western edge of a large area of first-class pine land, rolling, and heavily timbered. There is clay within two or three feet of the surface and lime rock from five to forty feet below the clay, beneath which is a quick sand affording a never failing supply of good water. Owing to the nearness of clay to the surface this region is specially adapted to the growth of pears, peaches, plums and grapes. Of these fruits there are now growing in the vicinity 15,000 pear trees, 1000 peach trees and an increasing number of persimmon and plum trees set in orchard. Vegetable growing is quite an industry, from 15,000 to 25,000 bushels of beans, cucumbers and tomatoes being annually shipped from this point, generally realizing good prices. Large crops of corn, cow peas, pinders, etc. are grown for home use, while cotton and syrup are the usual staples. The whole section is regarded as remarkably healthy.

BARTRAM is located in the high pine lands in the southwestern part of the County. The nearest railroad station is Bronson, on the Florida Railway and Navigation Company's line.

CAMPVILLE is situated on the Florida Railway and Navigation Company's line, five miles from Hawthorne, and nine miles from Waldo, on that high rolling ridge of land lying between Newnansville and Santa Fe lake. The population is about two hundred and fifty. It has one church, three stores, a literary society, a good school, a saw mill, and brick yard with a daily capacity of 50,000 brick. Where seven years ago, nothing but pine trees and wire grass grew, now there are over one hundred and fifty acres covered with beautiful orange, pear, peach and other fruit trees. The land is highly adapted to farming purposes, such as growing sugar cane, corn, oats, Sea-Island cotton and all kinds of vegetables, and is capable of being brought to a high state of cultivation, as it is of such a nature as to retain all manures not required to grow the crops, being what is known as a light gray soil, underlaid with a yellow subsoil to the depth of about two feet and then good solid clay. The best of all that is claimed for this section is its healthfulness.

EARLETON is beautifully located on the west shore of Lake Santa Fe. Being situated on a high ridge some two hundred feet above sea level, it is favored with a good breeze from the ocean, which not only makes it a healthy place but also enables the people to pass the summer months without suffering much from the heat. It has a daily mail, also daily communication with Waldo and Melrose by steamer. Visitors will find this place provided with a good hotel, general store, school and church. Sportsmen find a good opportunity to enjoy black bass fishing and duck shooting. Quail and other game are also plentiful. Some of the finest and largest orange, peach and Le Conte pear trees can be seen in and around the place. There is also a large business done in raising early vegetables and strawberries for the Northern market. Within the past few years the raising of grapes, both native and foreign varieties, has been very successfully tried. Not only have grapes brought good prices in the market but also the wine made from them is of an excellent quality. Earleton is about four miles southeast of Waldo, and within six miles of Melrose.

EVINSTON is an incorparated town on the Florida Southern Railway. It has one store, depot, post office, telegraph office, express office, two churches, a classical school and private boarding houses. The surrounding country is very fertile. Vegetables of every variety and general field crops are grown in great abundance. Oranges, peaches, grapes, pears and plums are successfully grown and attain great perfection.

FAIRBANKS.—This picturesque little town is located about six miles northeast of Gainesville, on the line of the Florida Railway and Navigation Company. One admirable feature of the town is its wide, straight streets, all beautifully planted with umbrageous trees ; for while the inhabitants would scoff at being termed lazy, they very sensibly believe in planting shade trees in the streets. It is surrounded with a fine, fertile country, all of which is well

33

adapted to the growth of the orange as well as vegetables and all tropical fruits Cotton, corn, oats, etc., are all cultivated with great success. Among the public improvements is a handsome Episcopal Church, of which denomination there is quite a strong and flourishing congregation. There is talk of erecting both Methodist and Presbyterian Churches in the near future. A free school also flourishes in this place, the attendance of pupils being large.

FORT FANNIN is located "'way down upon de S'wannee ribber," in the western extremity of the county. The country is sparsely settled, game is abundant, and some of the finest timbered lands in the county are to be found in this locality.

FRANKLAND, in the western part of the county, is in the midst of splendid yellow pine timber. The lands are well adapted to the growth of corn, cotton, peas, sugar-cane, etc. Oranges, peaches, figs, persimmons and the other fruits succeed well. The range for stock is excellent and game abundant; some of the finest lime rock is found in this locality. There are at Frankland post-office, store, saw and grist-mill and cotton-gins.

GAINESVILLE, the County seat of Alachua County and one of the most important interior towns of the State, has a population of about five thousand persons, whose hospitality and social qualities are all that could be desired. In point of health it has no superior in the State. On every hand are seen unquestionable evidences of the rapid development of the material interests of the city, in the center of which stands the Court House, one of the largest and handsomest in the State. The church facilities are ample and afford the best possible evidence of a religious and moral people. The wholesale trade, although in its infancy, shows unmistakable evidence of the fact that it is likely to grow speedily into large proportions. The importance of Gainesville as an educational center, commercial center, railroad center and as a place of residence, has and will continue to attract attention. Compared with a few years ago it is a new city. A majority of the business houses are substantial brick buildings and many of the private residences will compare favorably with those in any other part of the South. The city is orderly and the community law-abiding, fraternal and enterprising.

The transportation facilities are excellent. Railroads run north, south, east and west from the city. First-class public and private schools afford superior educational advantages. The United States Land Office is also located in this city. The lands around Gainesville are equal in productiveness to any in the State.

GORDON is situated a little to the east of La Crosse, and the soil partakes of the characteristics of that locality. The people are principally farmers, and generally prosperous.

GRACY is a station on the Savannah, Florida and Western Railway, about twenty miles northwest of Gainesville; has a sawmill, store and several dwelling houses. It is the center of a finely-timbered pine country.

GROVE PARK, a station and post-office on the Florida Southern Railway, fifteen miles from Gainesville, has a population of 250, two stores, hotel,

WILD PINE LANDS.

schoolhouse, church, saw and planing mill ; it is regularly laid out in blocks with streets 60 to 80 feet wide, well graded, and on many of them are set live oak trees. The soil in the vicinity is of good quality, a dark gray sandy loam, with clay subsoil ranging from 10 inches to 5 feet below the surface. This locality is noted for its healthfulness.

HAGUE is a new town situated on the Savannah, Florida and Western Railway, eleven miles northwest of Gainesville and five miles south of Newnansville, the new and old county seats of Alachua County. It contains a depot, express office, post-office, three stores and three churches. The people are moral and industrious, and are zealous supporters of education. The health is as good as in any part of the State. Tropical fruits, such as oranges, bananas, Japan persimmons and grape fruit mature well, and

35

peaches, pears, plums, cherries, grapes, mulberries and huckleberries grow in fine quality and quantity. Vegetable culture pays exceedingly well. From this station more vegetables are shipped to the Northern markets than from any other point between Gainesville and Savannah. Stock range is excellent; hogs and cattle do well the year round, and with but little feed they can be kept in fine condition through the winter. The timber in this section is of great variety and fine quality. All the trees of Florida and, indeed, of most of the States, can be found represented. Two large lumber mills do a very fine business. An abundance of sand, lime and fossiliferous rock is found in this section, the latter of which could be utilized.

HAMMOCK RIDGE, four miles southwest of Gainesville, on the line of the Florida Railway and Navigation Company, is in the midst of one of the finest vegetable sections in the county. It has been claimed, and it is believed to be absolutely true, that no point in the State produces as many vegetables from the same area of land, and none plant as many acres as in this immediate locality. The people are industrious and find their business of vegetable growing to be very profitable.

HAWTHORNE is situated at the junction of the Florida Southern and Florida Railway and Navigation Company's Railroads, nineteen miles east of Gainesville and fourteen miles south of Waldo, one hundred and forty-four feet above the St. Johns river at Palatka, and ninety feet above the celebrated Orange Lake, a short distance south. Within a radius of twenty miles lie numerous wild orange groves, forming nearly a circle around the town. All the necessaries and conveniences of life are to be had at Hawthorne. Double daily mails, two lines of telegraph, hotels, stores of several classes, ginning and manufacturing establishments, a photograph gallery, nursery, two livery stables, marble dealer, land and insurance agents, painters, carpenters, etc., represent the leading business interests of the town. A good number of public schools and the Hawthorne Academy furnish educational facilities. The Baptist, Methodist and Presbyterian are the leading religious denominations.

The lands lying east of the town are high and rolling, with small bodies of rich hammock lying along the shores of the many fine lakes near at hand. On the west the lands are lower and more level, but affording sites for many good farms and fine orange groves. Magnesia Springs, on the west, and Orange Springs, on the south, are accessible from this point, and are well known for their healing virtues. The rolling character of this region is shown by the six water mills now in operation, and other mill sites not yet improved.

ISLAND GROVE is a station and post-office on the Florida Railway and Navigation Company's Railroad, situated on the extreme southern line of the county. It has two stores and one saw mill. It is on an island, which is seven miles long and two miles wide. The lands are pine and hammock of fine quality, growing fine crops of oranges, corn, cotton and vegetables. From this island about ten thousand boxes of oranges and ten thousand crates of vegetables are annually shipped. Churches and schools are convenient.

JONESVILLE is sixteen miles west of Gainesville, midway between the

A CYPRESS SWAMP.

Savannah, Florida and Western and the Florida Railway and Navigation Company's Railroads. The Gainesville and Tallahassee road is expected to be constructed through the place. The lands are fertile and produce well cotton, corn, tobacco, potatoes and, in fact, all kinds of fruits and vegetables grown in other sections of the county. In this locality begins that vast territory of pine timber as yet in its virgin state. This section is particularly healthy, containing no prairies nor ponds to produce malaria. The people are hospitable and industrious, and extend a cordial welcome to all good permanent settlers.

KANAPAHA, a station and post-office on the Florida Railway and Navigation Company's road, west of Arredondo, is surrounded by a good pine country.

LA CROSSE is situated almost due north of Gainesville and about sixteen miles distant. It is in a beautiful and rich agricultural section, hammock and pine lands interspersed. This vicinity only lacks railroad facilities to bring it prominently into notice and to secure to its inhabitants abundant riches.

LOCHLOOSA, a landing and shipping point upon the lake of the same name, is also a station and post office on the Florida Railway and Navigation Company's line, about twenty-nine miles south of Waldo.

MAGNESIA SPRINGS, about fifteen miles south of Gainesville, and one mile from Grove Park, a station on the Florida Southern Railway, is noted for its celebrated Magnesia Springs, the medicinal virtues of which are well known for kidney complaints, diabetes, etc.; also noted for its natural fertilizer, in phosphatic rocks, millions of tons of which abound.

MELROSE is prettily located on the southwestern border of Santa Fe lake; a little bay makes in, creating a delightful and secluded water resort, where bathing, fishing and boating may be enjoyed. There are several stores and other industries, two Churches, Baptist and Episcopal, School house, two public squares and several fine residences. The land about Melrose is especially adapted for orange growing, while the lakes near by serve as a protection from frost.

MAYFIELD, post office and station on the Savannah, Florida and Western Railway, five and a half miles north of Gainesville. Lands are now being cleared at this point for the planting of one hundred acres in orange and other fruit trees by an incorporated company.

MICANOPY is situated near the southern boundary line of Alachua County, on the north side of Tuscawilla lake, about fifteen miles from Gainesville, and on a spur of the Florida Southern Railway. It bears the name of one of the greatest chiefs of the Seminole Indians. It was formerly an Indian settlement, and the home of old King Payne, Micanopy, Osceola, and other noted Indian chiefs, until the white people became their conquerors and appropriated it to themselves. The surrounding country is high and rolling and mostly hammock. All the farm crops of Florida, such as corn, oats, sugar-cane, cotton, etc., grow and fruit well on this soil. Truck farming is conducted on an extensive and profitable scale. This vicinity is

38

the home of the orange, the native or wild trees having been found there. Some of the largest and most profitable orange groves are located in and around the town. Micanopy has three white, Methodist, Baptist and Presbyterian, and three colored Churches. A private Classical and Mathematical School and a public School are in a flourishing condition.

NEWNANSVILLE is about one mile from Alachua Station, on the Savannah, Florida and Western Railway, and is the oldest town in Alachua County. The surrounding country is second to none in the State and is well adapted to the growth of nearly all the cereals and fruits of a semi-tropical climate. The soil of the high hills for the most part is clay mixed with gravel, underlying a thin but rich loam. The country is covered with a heavy growth of pine, hickory, live oak, white oak, magnolia and other trees, and is well watered by springs and clear water lakes. This is one of the most picturesque portions of Florida. The society is good. Merchants are enterprising, and churches and schools convenient. Newnansville was the county seat of Alachua County until 1856, when the Court House was moved to Gainesville by a vote of the people.

NEW GAINESVILLE is an addition of and adjoins the city of Gainesville on the east. Situated on high pine land, overlooking the business portion of the City, with excellent water, broad streets, good soil for gardens and groves, in close proximity to churches and schools, and on the line of the Gainesville City and Suburban street railway, it is indeed a most excellent and beautiful site for residences. In the center of the plot is a park in which it is proposed to erect a large hotel. Adjoining the town are lots of level pine land well suited to the growth of oranges, peaches and pears or the cultivation of vegetables or farm crops.

NORTH GAINESVILLE is a suburb of the city of Gainesville, extending one and a half miles north of the city limits. The citizens are prosperous truck growers and raise large quantities of strawberries and vegetables for market. There is not a more pleasant settlement or a better class of citizens to be found anywhere. They are honest, enterprising and industrious, and their homes are the admiration of visitors.

ORANGE HEIGHTS, on the Florida Railway and Navigation Co.'s road, sixty-five miles south of Jacksonville, is nicely located on gently rolling land. The town is scarcely two years old, has about 300 inhabitants, three stores, one hotel, express office, photographer, church, school house, blacksmith shop, cotton gin, novelty works, saw and planing mill. The population embraces representatives from most every state in the Union, and are an intelligent, sober and energetic people. The soil is a dark pine with a large per cent. of humus and is well adapted to the successful growing of fruits, sugarcane, rice and vegetables.

ORION, on the Savanah, Florida and Western Railway, twenty-three miles north of Gainesville, has a population of about 150—four general stores, one saw-mill, one cotton gin, one blacksmith shop, two churches, public schools, and one hotel. The land is high and dry, and the pine timber good. A great many hard stone are to be found in this section, and hundreds of carloads have been and are now being carried from this point to be utilized on the jetties at the mouth of the St. Johns river. The post office at this station is called Santeffey, from the name of the river which flows near it.

PALMER, formerly known as Batonville, lies midway between Arredondo and Archer, on the Florida Railroad and Navigation Company's line, and is surrounded by a high, dry pine country.

PARADISE is a new town four miles north of Gainesville on the Savannah, Florida and Western Railway. A birds-eye view of this town would show high rolling pine land, with three beautiful streams of water meandering from north to south in a southeasterly direction, the margin of each stream being lined with oak, hickory, magnolia, gum, bay, ash and cherry; also persimmon trees and wild grape vines in abundance. This was one of the first sections entered in the Arredondo Grant, over fifty years ago, when people had the choice of all the lands in this vicinity, showing conclusively that they considered nothing better. A portion of this section, some 250 acres, has been under cultivation the past thirty or forty years, and about that time one of the beautiful fields was called Paradise, hence the name of Paradise Station.

Persons desiring to make a home, and wishing to raise a diversity of crops and fruits, will certainly be fully satisfied by coming to Paradise, as it has been demonstrated that no better lands can be found in the State for the production of strawberries, oranges, peaches, pears, etc. Although this town is less than three years old it has twenty residences already occupied. There is also a station house on the railroad, post office and public school house. An intelligent physician who has resided in the town for two years, says that he can cheerfully recommend the place as being freer from malaria and chills and fever than any place he knows of in the South.

ROCHELLE, at the junction of the main branch with the Southern division of the Florida Southern Railway, is a thriving little town of about one hundred and seventy-five inhabitants ten miles from Gainesville; has a hotel, two schools, two churches, two general stores, cotton and grist mill. It is surrounded by many profitable vegetable farms; twenty-four trains on the Florida Southern Railway pass this point daily.

RUTLEDGE.—This is a new town five miles west of Gainesville on the line of the Gainesville, Tallahassee and Western Railroad, and three miles from Paradise station on the Savannah Florida and Western Railway. Three stores, a post-office, a large boarding-house, a few comfortable dwellings, a dozen or more buildings altogether, as yet constitute the town. The beautiful rolling land and rich hammock soil, combined with unusual healthfulness, has highly commended this section to all who have examined it. As a temporary retreat in winter or as a permanent residence it offers advantages particularly to the Northern or Western farmer, for here he finds soil that is really suited for general farming as well as for mere gardening or fruit raising. Some of the finest tobacco was grown here last season that was ever raised in the State. Corn, oats, rye, cotton, tobacco, sugar-cane, as well as all the fruits and vegetables are raised in abundance. Both natural and cultivated grasses do well and afford good feed the year round for stock. Probably some of the best grade of cattle in the county will be found in this neighborhood.

SUTHERLAND, a station on the Florida Railway and Navigation Railroad, between Arredondo and Archer, is surrounded by a good high pine country.

TACOMA.—Lying between Alachua lake on the north, affording excellent water protection, and Levy lake on the South, is situated a cluster of small farms of from ten to forty or more acres, locally known as Tacoma. Several

A FLORIDA LAKE SHORE.

hundred acres of fine orange groves flourishing and well-cared for are situated in this locality. Large quantities of vegetables are shipped from this settlement *via* Micanopy, the post-office town, distant from three to six miles.

TRENTON, formerly known as Joppa, is about twenty-five miles west of Gainesville, in a rich country of beautiful rolling pine land, some of it the best in the county for the production of Sea-Island cotton.

WALDO, the second town in importance in the county, occupies an important position as the junction of the Southern with the Central Division of the Florida Railway and Navigation Railroad, and is destined to be a place of importance. Although the place looks flat and level it is one hundred and fifty feet above the sea level by actual measurement. East of the town lies a perfect net-work of lakes, large and small, which gives to the country round about its significant name of the Central Lake Region of the State. Lying but a few miles distant to the east is Lake Santa Fe, the largest, and between it and Waldo is Lake Alto, considerably smaller. The Sante Fe Canal, from Waldo into and across Lake Alto and thence into Lake Santa Fe, gives access by means of a steamer to one of the finest agricultural sections of the State. The shore line thus reached is some thirty miles in extent, and embraces connection with Melrose, at the eastern extremity of the lake, from whence to Green Cove Springs, on the St. Johns river, a line of railway is in course of construction. It is a fact no less remarkable than well authenticated that the orange groves in the vicinity of Waldo have scarcely suffered from the effects of the severe cold spells which have visited the State during the past few years. This apparent immunity from frost has been no doubt truly attributed to the presence of natural protection, such as bodies of water, forests, etc.

The soil in this vicinity is a dark, sandy loam, underlaid with red clay, well adapted to the growth of grapes and specially suited for the growth of all semi-tropical fruits that are adapted to the climate. Nowhere in the

ORANGE GROVE AND RESIDENCE.

State will finer or better orange groves be found than can be seen around Waldo. Japan plums, Japan persimmons and grapes of both European and native varieties all flourish well and reward the orchardist and horticulturist with splendid crops every year. The water is pure free stone, clear and sparkling, no admixture of lime or foreign substance of any kind. The health of the place is unsurpassed. Malarial fevers rare, chills and fevers unknown. No epidemic has ever raged in the town; twice has yellow fever been brought there and in each instance it was confined to the patients that came with it. After this experience, it is needless to add, that with the elevation, pure air and clear sparkling water, the most timid need have nothing to fear

42

in this locality on the score of health. Waldo has six stores, seven churches, white and colored, three public and one private school. A cold storage warehouse is now being constructed at a cost of about $50,000. The railroad now being constructed from Macon, Georgia, to Palatka will pass through Waldo, giving to the town and vicinity a competing transportation line.

WINDSOR is situated on the east bank of Lake Newnan, a charming lake, twenty-five miles in circumference, surrounded by semi-tropical scenery and abounding in fish. It is ten miles east of Gainesville and lies between the railroad stations—Rochelle, on the Florida Southern, three miles south, and Camp-

SAIL BOATS ON A FLORIDA LAKE.

ville, on the Florida Railway and Navigation Road three miles east. Another recent railroad survey, a branch of the Jacksonville and Gulf Air Line, goes right through the town. By steamer on the lake, communication may be had with Gainesville. The town is only three years old, has about sixty residences, two stores, one drug store, one flourishing school with two teachers, one Methodist church, two saw and planing-mills, and one large tub and pail factory. Windsor is in a good farming and vegetable region and first-class fruit land. As adjuncts for a beautiful home, the water-oak and live-oak grow here to great proportions and beautiful grassy lawns can be grown of Bermuda grass. The town has beautiful oak-shaded avenues, upon which are choice lots for quiet, restful homes with orchards and gardens.

YULEE is a station and post-office on the Florida Railway and Navigation Railroad, between Gainesville and Waldo, five miles south-west of the latter place.

CONCLUSION.

After a thorough investigation of the material resources of the State of Florida, and particularly of the County of Alachua, the assertion is made without the fear of contradiction that can be substantiated, that there is no State in the Union where an industrious poor man or a man of limited means can more easily acquire a prosperous home and live comfortably with less exertion, or where capital may be invested with certainty of larger profits than in the State of Florida; and while not disposed to draw any invidious distinction between Alachua and other Counties in the State, it is insisted that no other locality offers greater and in very many respects equal advantages.

The statistics show that more money per acre is realized from Florida in crops from its cultivated area, than from any other similarly sized territory in the country. The soil of Florida has been considered poor, but many sections are as rich as can be found elsewhere, and even the poor lands respond to judicious fertilizing in a way that is amazing.

In Florida, Nature works with the farmer. She gives him a genial climate and the whole year for a season; she sends him rain just when he most requires it, and permits no drought at all; snow and ice never come to injure or delay his work; he needs no cellars and he therefore builds none; the months of enforced idleness and wasted time that burden the Northern farmer and consume his substance are not within the Floridian's experience.

While many who come to Florida succeed without capital to start with, yet he who can bring a few hundred or a few thousand dollars will have a great advantage. So large a proportion of the penniless class have rushed to the "Land of Flowers" that there is hardly enough capital to keep them always employed, hence the grievous and gloomy letters that find their way into Northern papers. Those looking for "genteel" positions, clerkships, etc., will be liable to disappointment in this or any other new country, but prosperity awaits the energetic and capable tiller of the soil or tradesman.

To the young, just starting upon the voyage of life, to the middle-aged and to the old, who may desire a home in a sunny clime, where health and prosperity may be secured, where the young before the meridian of life may feel assured of a home, where the middle-aged may make such provision for himself and family as to feel that his declining years are provided for, and where the old may put on a new lease of life amid the orange groves of a salubrious clime, the advice is given, come to Alachua and investigate the advantages which she offers.

45

SAVANNAH,

FLORIDA AND WESTERN

RAILWAY,

—— THE FAMOUS ——

WAYCROSS SHORT LINE

—— AND ——

FLORIDA DISPATCH LINE.

The Shortest, Quickest and Best Route

for Passengers and Freight to and from Jacksonville, Gainesville and all points in Florida.

FOUR EXPRESS PASSENGER TRAINS DAILY.

FAST FREIGHT SERVICE BY EXPRESS TRAINS.

C. D. OWENS, Traffic Man.   WM. P. HARDEE, Gen. Frt. and Pass. Agt.
W. M. DAVIDSON, Gen. Traffic Agt. for Florida.

Florida Fertilizer M'f'g Co.,

MANUFACTURERS OF

HIGH GRADE

BONE FERTILIZERS.

OFFICE AND WORKS,

GAINESVILLE, FLORIDA.

BONES.

The Florida Fertilizer Manufacturing Company will pay in cash the highest market price for all

CLEAN AND DRY BONES,

delivered at their works in Gainesville, Florida.   No green bones wanted.

WE INVITE CORRESPONDENCE UPON THE SUBJECT.

PHILLIP   MILLER,

—— WHOLESALE AND RETAIL DEALER IN ——

GROCERIES,

FEED AND ——

—— PROVISIONS,

Gainesville, Florida.

48

49

DAILY MORNING RECORD,

PUBLISHED BY THE

❈ RECORD PUBLISHING COMPANY, ❈

GAINESVILLE, FLORIDA.

$5.00 PER ANNUM.

FLORIDA RECORD,

The Leading Weekly of Alachua County.

$1.00 PER ANNUM.

The best advertising mediums in existence for reaching the people of Central Florida, the garden spot of the State. Alive, progressive, soundly democratic and up with the times, their circulation exceeds that of all other county papers combined.

With the finest office in Florida, the only steam power press in the county, and one of the best in the State and with a job office stocked and equipped bountifully and with the best of material, we are prepared to meet all demands.

Sample copies free. Address

RECORD PUBLISHING CO., . . GAINESVILLE, FLA.

GAINESVILLE NURSERIES.

ESTABLISHED IN 1878.

All leading varieties of fruit trees suitable to Florida soil and climate in stock. NEW FRUITS A SPECIALTY. Prices reasonable. Circulars free on application. Address,

PORTER & CESSNA, Managers, Gainesville, Fla.

❈ EAST FLORIDA NURSERIES. ❈

GEO. B. CELLON, Manager,

GAINESVILLE, FLORIDA.

Peaches, Plums, Pears and Persimmons (Japan) in quantities to suit purchasers, at LOWEST CASH PRICES. Best varieties of Strawberry Plants also in stock.

CATALOGUE FREE.

L. K. RAWLINS,

REAL ESTATE & LOANS.

ONLY SET OF ABSTRACT BOOKS IN ALACHUA COUNTY.

Office, Court House,

GAINESVILLE, . . . FLORIDA.

VALUABLE LANDS FOR SALE AT A SACRIFICE.

5,000 acres of rich Pine and Hammock Lands, situated in the best farming and fruit growing section of the State, comprising several small farms under cultivation and some of the best oak and hickory timbered lands in Florida. All lying in and around Newnansville, fifteen miles north of Gainesville, in Alachua county. Land peculiarly adapted to the vegetable and fruit culture, and will be sold on easy terms and at a great bargain. For further information call on or address,

F. P OLMSTEAD,   Or, G. P. OLMSTEAD.
    Newnansville, Fla.   Gainesville, Fla.

A SPLENDID OPPORTUNITY TO GET A MODEL FLORIDA HOME,

at a low price if purchased at once, in the Orange Belt and Clear Lake Region. The House has eighteen large, airy rooms with fire places, and a double veranda extends entirely around the house. One hour's ride from Palatka, the same distance from Gainesville. Nine acres of land with Barn, Store House and Out Buildings will be sold with the property. For further information call on or address,

D. E. COOPER, . . Gainesville, Florida.

VALUABLE FARM.

For sale, an improved farm of 40 acres, situated five miles west of Gainesville, three miles from Railroad Station. Rich hammock land, fenced; two two-story dwellings, store and post office; barn, stables, tools, stock, etc., all complete; orange grove set out. For terms etc., address,

F. B. DUNHAM, . . . Gainesville, Florida.

BEFORE SETTLING IN FLORIDA, BE SURE TO VISIT

❈ WINDSOR. ❈

Very healthy. Beautifully situated on Lake Newnan. Choice lots, Fruit and Vegetable lands cheap.

Strangers visiting Windsor must not confound the town proper, where post office and public school are, with any suburban addition claiming the same name.

For full particulars address either,

W. J. WALKER,   G. W. KELLEY,
    J. L. KELLEY,   G. D. WATSON,

WINDSOR, FLORIDA.

FLORIDA FRUIT AND INVESTMENT COMPANY,

GAINESVILLE, FLORIDA.

CAPITAL, $100.000.

DR. J. A. McDONALD, Pres., Boston, Mass.

·   GEO. H. SUTHERLAND, Sec., Gainesville, Fla.

S. W. TROWBRIDGE, Treas., 5 Court St., Boston, Mass.

A RARE CHANCE FOR INVESTMENT.

ENORMOUS DIVIDENDS ASSURED.

Send to either Secretary or Treasurer for Circular.

WINDSOR FLORIDA

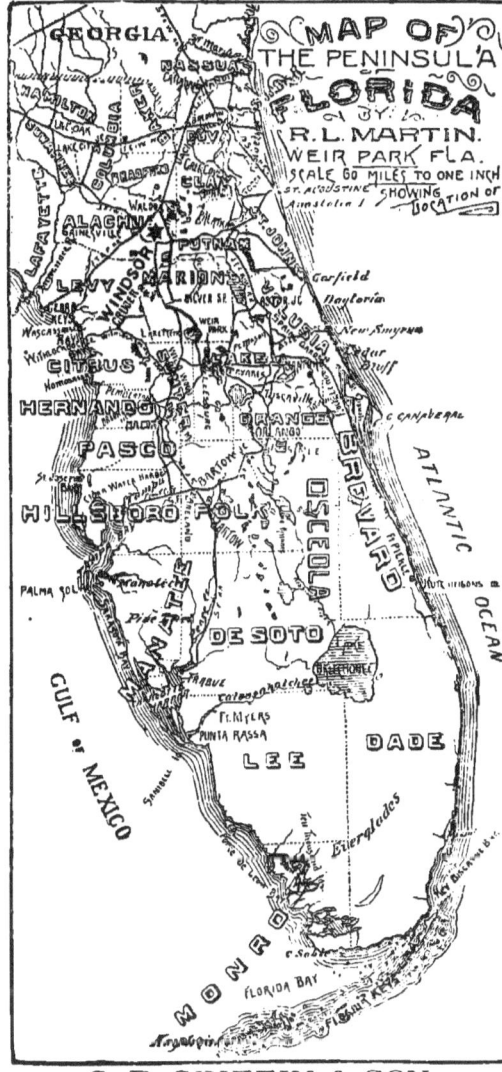

is one of the prettiest and healthiest places in the State, with a population of about four hundred, and containing eighty houses, four stores, two saw mills, two planing mills, a large tub and pail factory, the only one in the State, two public halls, one church. Broad streets, set with shade trees, add wonderfully to its natural beauty. It is located in Alachua county, one of the best counties (if not the best) in the State. It is remarkably healthy, has good water, and the land is superior to most in the State, well adapted to the growth of the orange, peach, quince, plum, fig and other small fruits; vegetables of most kinds do remarkably well here and are raised largely for shipment and local markets. The beautiful Lake Newnan, some thirty miles in circumference, affords a great abundance of fine fish, and an excellent opportunity for boating, hunting, etc.

If you want a home in Florida, where you can have health and raise something to live on, we would invite you to visit Windsor. To do so, call at our office in Hubbard Block, Pine street, Jacksonville, and get a ticket either to Rochelle, on the Florida Southern Railway or to Campville, on the Florida Railway and Navigation Co's line, either running some three miles distant.

Land, either cleared or timbered, can be had in large or small tracts at moderate prices, and fine large lots in the village for building. We will make this remarkable offer: To any one who will build a house to cost not less than $1,000, we will donate a fine lot of about one acre, worth $500. We think if you will take the trouble to come and see us you will be pleased with Windsor.

For any further information address,

G. B. GRIFFIN & SON,
either at Jacksonville or Windsor.

BIRD'S-EYE VIEW OF ALACHUA COUNTY FLORIDA